www.BillieBBrownBooks.com

Billie B. Brown Books

The Bad Butterfly
The Soccer Star
The Midnight Feast
The Second-best Friend
The Extra-special Helper
The Beautiful Haircut
The Big Sister
The Spotty Vacation
The Birthday Mix-up
The Secret Message
The Little Lie
The Best Project
The Deep End
The Copycat Kid
The Night Fright

First American Edition 2014
Kane Miller, A Division of EDC Publishing

Text copyright © 2011 Sally Rippin
Illustrations copyright © 2011 Aki Fukuoka
Logo and design copyright © 2011 Hardie Grant Egmont

First published in Australia in 2011 by Hardie Grant Egmont

For information contact:
Kane Miller, A Division of EDC Publishing
P.O. Box 470663
Tulsa, OK 74147-0663
www.kanemiller.com
www.edcpub.com
www.usbornebooksandmore.com

Library of Congress Control Number: 2013944864

Printed and bound in the United States of America
12 13 14 15 16 17 18 19
ISBN: 978-1-61067-256-6

Billie B. Brown

The Secret Message

By Sally Rippin

Illustrated by Aki Fukuoka

Kane Miller
A DIVISION OF EDC PUBLISHING

Chapter One

Billie B. Brown has
one bathing suit, seven
seashells and a pail and
shovel. Do you know
what the "B" in Billie B.
Brown stands for?

Beach!

It is summer vacation and Billie B. Brown is at the beach.

Today Billie is going to make a sand castle. She is going to make the biggest, most beautiful sand castle you have ever seen.

Seven seashells

A pail and shovel

One
bathing
suit

Billie's mom reads a book under a beach umbrella. Her dad reads the newspaper. Sometimes they even fall asleep. Can you imagine? They are absolutely no fun at all!

Billie puts on some sunscreen and sits out in the sun.

She starts to build a sand castle. There's a family with two girls nearby. The girls are building a sand castle too. Their sand castle is very big and very beautiful.

Billie feels a teensy bit **jealous**. She wishes her best friend, Jack, was here to help her.

"Lunch!" Billie's mom calls.

Just in time. Billie's tummy

is growling like a tiger!

Billie trudges up the beach to sit in the shade. Billie's mom gives her a sandwich. Even though Billie has wiped her hands, her banana sandwich still tastes **crunchy**.

Billie's dad says, "Would you like extra sand in your witch?"

He says that every time they eat lunch at the beach, but Billie still laughs.

Billie watches the other girls make their castle. One of them looks about the same age as Billie.

She has red hair and freckles and she is wearing a pink-and-white polka-dot bathing suit. Billie wishes *she* had a fancy suit.

"Why don't you ask if you can play with them?" Billie's mom says.

Billie shakes her head. She feels shy.

She would love to play with those kids, but she is too **scared** to go over and ask them.

What if they don't want to play with me? Billie thinks.

What if they laugh at me or they are mean?

No, Billie decides. *It is much safer just to play on my own.*

Chapter Two

Billie finishes her
sandwich and goes
back to her sand castle.
She decides that it needs
a moat. Billie digs and
digs and digs.

Her shovel hits something hard. **Clink!** Billie reaches into the hole. She feels something smooth.

Billie digs deeper and pulls out a tiny bottle. It is as green as the sea and as small as her hand.

Billie holds the bottle up to the sun.

The glass is so dark that it is impossible to see what's inside.

A girl walks past collecting shells. She sees the bottle in Billie's hand.

"Ooh!" she says.
"What's inside?"

Billie shrugs. "I don't
know," she says.

"It's beautiful,"
says the little girl.
She reaches out her
sandy fingers to touch
the green glass.

"I'm Billie," says Billie.

"I'm Charlotte," the
little girl says. "That's
my sister, Harriet." She
points to the girl in the
fancy bathing suit.

Harriet, Billie thinks.

That's a nice name.

Then she has an idea.
A super-duper idea.

"Actually, I think
there's a secret message
inside the bottle,"
Billie whispers to
Charlotte. "It's probably
from a pirate."

"Wow!" says Charlotte.
Her eyes open wide.
"I have to tell Harriet!
She loves pirates!"

Billie watches Charlotte
run along the beach to
where Harriet is waiting.

Chapter Three

That afternoon, Billie and her mom and dad walk to the shops to buy ice cream. Billie always chooses banana chocolate chip with sprinkles.

Billie has to eat her
ice cream very quickly
so that it doesn't melt.
Already it is drip-drip-
dripping on her toes.

Billie walks back to the
beach and finishes her
ice cream. When she looks
up, there is a girl standing
in front of her. It's Harriet.
Billie's heart begins to flap
around like a butterfly.

"My sister told me you
found a bottle with a
message inside," says
Harriet. "Can I see?"

Billie pulls the bottle out of her pocket.

Harriet squints at the dark glass. "I can't see any message inside," she frowns.

"It has to be very small," Billie says. "To fit in the bottle."

"Hmm," Harriet says. "Who do you think wrote it?"

Billie shrugs. She feels a little bit **shy**. "Probably a pirate."

Harriet smiles. "Or maybe a *princess*?" she says. "Captured by pirates?"

"Or maybe the prince trying to save her?" says Billie excitedly. "But his boat has sunk and now he's stuck on a desert island!"

"Yeah!" Harriet says. "Hey, do you want to come and help us build our sand castle?"

Billie looks at her mom and dad.

"Sure!" says Billie's dad.

"Let me put some more sunscreen on you first," says Billie's mom.

Billie wiggles as her mom covers her in sunscreen. Then she runs after Harriet to the big, beautiful sand castle. Charlotte is waiting for them there.

Billie holds the little bottle in her hands. The girls all try to guess what's inside.

Billie feels very special
to have found such a
magical thing.

Then Billie has an idea.
Carefully she balances
the little green bottle on
top of the sand castle.
It looks magnificent!
Now it is the biggest,
most beautiful sand castle
on the beach.

Charlotte jumps up and
down excitedly. Harriet
does a handstand.
Billie decides she will do
a handstand too.

But she is not used to
doing handstands on the
soft sand. She wibbles
and wobbles, then…
crash! Billie falls down.
Right on top of the big,
beautiful sand castle!

Harriet and Charlotte gasp.

Billie stands up quickly.
But it is too late. The
sand castle is ruined.

Billie stares at the crushed sand castle. Right in the middle is her little green bottle. It has cracked neatly in half. The girls kneel down to look at it.

And that's when they see…there is nothing inside it. Nothing at all.

Billie covers her face with her hands. Big fat tears roll down her cheeks. She grabs the two pieces of the bottle and runs back to her mom and dad.

Chapter Four

Billie has decided that
this is the worst day ever.
She has made a sand castle
and broken a sand castle.
She has found a bottle and
broken a bottle.

Worst of all, she made
a friend, but now she is
sure the friendship will
be broken.

Harriet knows there
wasn't any message
in the bottle. Billie was
just making up stories.
Harriet will never
want to be friends with
Billie now!

Billie sits on her towel under the beach umbrella and cries.

"Why don't you just say sorry?" Billie's mom suggests.

Billie shakes her head.
She is much too **scared**
to go and talk to those
girls now. Especially after
everything she has done!

Billie B. Brown is
good at lots of things.
She is good at the
monkey bars and she is
good at building forts.

She is good at soccer
and she is good at
midnight feasts. But the
thing that Billie B. Brown
is best at is coming up
with good ideas.

Billie wipes her eyes.
She looks at the little
broken bottle in her hand.
And then she has an idea.

It is the superest-duperest
idea she has had all day!

Can you guess what
Billie is thinking?

Billie tears off a corner
of her dad's newspaper.
Then she takes his pencil
and writes in very small
writing.

Dear Princess Harriet,

I am really sorry I broke your
sand castle. Can I help you build
a new one? If you want to be
my friend, please send me back
a message.

From Captain Billie

Billie rolls the message up tightly and puts it inside one half of the bottle. She puts the other half of the bottle on top. Then she takes a hair elastic and wraps it around the two halves. It holds the message inside perfectly.

Billie waits for Harriet and Charlotte to go for a swim.

She runs over and puts the
bottle on Harriet's towel.
Then she runs back.

Harriet gets out of the
water first. She picks up her
towel. Billie sees the little
green bottle drop onto the
sand. Harriet picks it up.

Billie holds her breath
and looks away. She can't
bear to watch!

Then Charlotte runs
toward Billie with
the bottle in her hand.
Billie opens
the bottle.
Her heart is
jumping up
and down.

But…oh dear!
The bottle is empty!
Billie hangs her head.

Harriet doesn't want to be her friend after all!

"Oh," says Charlotte. "I forgot. Princess Harriet said she'd love to be your friend. She also said sorry that there's no message, but she didn't have a pen and paper."

Billie bursts out laughing.

It's not the worst day ever, it's the best day ever! Billie is on the beach, the sun is shining and, best of all, she has a brand-new friend!

Collect them all!

The Bad Butterfly
By Sally Rippin

The Soccer Star
By Sally Rippin

The Midnight Feast
By Sally Rippin

The Second-best Friend
By Sally Rippin

The Extra-special Helper
By Sally Rippin

The Beautiful Haircut
By Sally Rippin

The Big Sister
By Sally Rippin

The Spotty Vacation
By Sally Rippin

The Birthday Mix-up
By Sally Rippin

The Secret Message
By Sally Rippin

The Little Lie
By Sally Rippin

The Best Project

The Deep End
By Sally Rippin

The Copycat Kid
By Sally Rippin

The Night Fright
By Sally Rippin